THE AMERICAN BALD EAGLE AND ME

Photography by Kristen L. Holmberg
Story by Fred B. Holmberg

The American Bald Eagle and Me

A story of an American Bald Eagle telling a young child about its life.

Photography by Kristen L. Holmberg
Story by Fred B. Holmberg

Graphic Design by Aikman Design, Kennebunk, Maine

Printed in the United States of America
Holmberg Publishing • Maine, USA
ISBN: 9798884321960

Email Kristen at schnookums@roadrunner.com

An American Bald Eagle
Flew down from the sky
Landed on a branch
Looked me straight in the eye

Why are you here?
I asked with a smile
Are you flying away or
Will you stay for awhile?

I saw you taking pictures
And thought you should know
Where I live, what I do
Where I come and where I go

Tell me, do tell me
I want to find out
Where you live, what you do,
What your life is about

I live in a house
Way up in that tree
You could call it a nest
That is OK with me

It's made out of wood
Smaller pieces to be sure
It's just like your home
And very secure

My children live there
As do I and my wife
You should come near and visit
It's a wonderful life

I have wings, you have arms,
I guess you can't fly like I do
Although I am very strong
I can't carry you

I fly really fast
So I will try to go really slow
Watch where I am
As you follow from below

So let's go to the seashore
So you can see what I eat
I catch fish in the water
Now that is pretty neat

I catch a fish
I have leftovers too
So I take them back home
But I don't make fish stew

Now you may ask
"Do you bathe in the sun?"
I pick myself clean
It really is quite fun

Watch a moment
And I will show you how,
First legs, then wings,
Then my body right now

I keep on going
Until each feather is done
Then I shake off my body
And dry in the sun

I must go home now
She is waiting for me
The chick she is watching
Opened her eyes and can see

So come back tomorrow
And I'll tell you some more
About the life of Bald Eagles
Who live by the shore

Some Interesting Facts for the Reader

The Bald Eagle is the official bird of the United States.

Its wing span is 5.9 to 7.5 feet.

Its life span is about twenty years.

It weighs 6.6 to 14 pounds.

In diving, it flies at a speed of 75 to 99 miles per hour.

Eagles mate in pairs, both of whom look after the young.

Kristen L. Holmberg is a photographer who lives in Maine. In her spare time, Kristen is roaming throughout Maine with her camera. She has discovered several spots where eagles tend to linger  in Southern Maine and is constantly photographing the majestic eagles. Her photographs have been published in the Maine Sunday Telegram, the Portland Press Herald and the Village magazine.

Fred B. Holmberg, Kristen's dad, also lives in Maine and has been writing since he was in grammar school. He has published three books of poems, co-authored a WWII fiftieth anniversary book, "Have You Forgotten," and  has written dozens of articles and prize-winning poems, some of which have been published in French, Spanish and Chinese. Holmberg also adapted the children's book, "Little Blue," from a non-verbal CD to book form.

Thank you mom!
I love you!

Made in United States
North Haven, CT
29 March 2024

50674780R00024